Streaker, the f[...]own, is in a spin . . .

and it's not because of all the Christmas decorations!

[C]an Trevor and his friend Tina help before [it]'s too late?

Jeremy Strong once worked in a bakery, putting the jam into three thousand doughnuts every night. Now he puts the jam in stories instead, which he finds much more exciting. At the age of three, he fell out of a first-floor bedroom window and landed on his head. His mother says that this damaged him for the rest of his life and refuses to take any responsibility. He loves writing stories because he says it is 'the only time you alone have complete control and can make anything happen'. His ambition is to make you laugh (or at least snuffle). Jeremy Strong lives near Bath with his wife, Gillie, four cats and a flying cow.

Are you feeling silly enough to read more?

LAUGH YOUR SOCKS OFF WITH

Jeremy STRONG

CHRISTMAS CHAOS for the Hundred-Mile-An-Hour Dog

Illustrated by Rowan Clifford

PUFFIN

PUFFIN BOOKS

Published by the Penguin Group
Penguin Books Ltd, 80 Strand, London WC2R 0RL, England
Penguin Group (USA) Inc., 375 Hudson Street, New York, New York 10014, USA
Penguin Group (Canada), 90 Eglinton Avenue East, Suite 700, Toronto, Ontario, Canada M4P 2Y3
(a division of Pearson Penguin Canada Inc.)
Penguin Ireland, 25 St Stephen's Green, Dublin 2, Ireland (a division of Penguin Books Ltd)
Penguin Group (Australia), 250 Camberwell Road, Camberwell, Victoria 3124, Australia
(a division of Pearson Australia Group Pty Ltd)
Penguin Books India Pvt Ltd, 11 Community Centre, Panchsheel Park, New Delhi – 110 017, India
Penguin Group (NZ), 67 Apollo Drive, Rosedale, Auckland 0632, New Zealand
(a division of Pearson New Zealand Ltd)
Penguin Books (South Africa) (Pty) Ltd, 24 Sturdee Avenue, Rosebank,
Johannesburg 2196, South Africa

Penguin Books Ltd, Registered Offices: 80 Strand, London WC2R 0RL, England

puffinbooks.com

First published 2009
This edition published 2011
001 – 10 9 8 7 6 5 4 3 2 1

Text copyright © Jeremy Strong, 2009
Illustrations copyright © Rowan Clifford, 2009
All rights reserved

The moral right of the author and illustrator has been asserted

Set in Baskerville MT
Printed in Great Britain by Clays Ltd, St Ives plc

British Library Cataloguing in Publication Data
A CIP catalogue record for this book is available from the British Library

ISBN: 978–0–141–32500–2

www.greenpenguin.co.uk

Happy Christmas to Sam and all readers

Contents

1. Lions 1, Elephants 0

Streaker is the best dog in the whole world.
That's what I think. Unfortunately nobody agrees
with me. Mum and Dad have handed her over to
me because they can't control her. I'm the only
one who can do that. Streaker will do anything
I say, but not necessarily when I actually say it.
If I shout 'Come here', she will do it, eventually,
although I might have to wait until the next day,
or maybe the day after.

However, she is BRILLIANT at doing all sorts
of other things. For example, she can:

1. Run like toast on fire. (The toast
has got legs, obviously.)

2. Leap like a kangaroo on an

iceberg. (Kanga is trying to get warm.)

3. Eat like Frogmouth Freddie. (He's in my class at school and I have seen him eat three jam doughnuts ALL AT THE SAME TIME. How disgusting is that?)

4. And, most of all, she is brilliant
at GETTING INTO TROUBLE.
Streaker has been in more trouble
than a room full of bank robbers.
In fact she has been in trouble
with Mum, Dad, me, my friend Tina,
Tina's mother, the police, the dog
warden and about half the people
in our town.

She's also pretty good at looking after her
puppies. She has got three pups and they are
called, in the following order: One, Two and
Three. Yes, I know – not exactly interesting
names, are they? I wanted to call them Piddle,
Tiddle and Widdle but Mum said NO WAY.

'They are not nice names, Trevor,' she
complained.

'They're not nice puppies,' I pointed out. 'Not
when they're tiddling and –'

'Stop,' Mum broke in sharply. 'No details, thank you very much. It's bad enough having to clean up their mess.'

'But you get me to do that,' I said.

'She's your dog,' Mum shot back.

'But they're Streaker's puppies, not mine. She should clean up after them.'

'She's a dog,' Mum went on. 'How often have you seen a dog with a mop and bucket?'

I shrugged. 'Maybe she could be trained.'

Mum gawped at me for a moment and then burst into laughter. 'You have got to be joking! That dog couldn't be trained to breathe, let alone do anything useful.'

'Mum, Streaker knows how to breathe and breathing happens to be *very* useful.'

'And you know perfectly well what I mean, smarty-pants. How many times have you tried to train her? How many times have you failed? The words "Streaker" and "training" just do not fit together.'

I have to admit Mum is probably right there.
I mean, Streaker doesn't even know her name!
Anyhow, Dad and Mum decided that since the
puppies would not be staying with us forever they
didn't need proper names and that's why they
ended up being called Boring, Boring and Boring.
Or to put it another way: One, Two and Three.

'They'll be ready to leave us just in time for
Christmas,' said Dad. 'Excellent.'

'But it will be their first ever Christmas!'
I protested. 'Can't we keep them? Please?'

Dad looked towards heaven as if he was
searching for help, but the help he got wasn't very
helpful as far as I was concerned. 'No,' Dad said
bluntly.

'I'll feed them,' I suggested and made my best pleading face.

'No,' Dad repeated. 'And stop trying to look like a dying idiot.'

I made my final offer. 'I'll buy them off you.'

Mum sighed. 'Trevor, puppies grow up. Soon they will be the same size as their mother, if not bigger. You haven't got the money to buy them or feed them and we haven't got room for them. We already have Streaker *and* Erik under our feet all day.'

In case you're wondering, Erik is the cat that Streaker brought home with her when she got lost a couple of months ago. (She also brought a manic baboon, but that's another story.) Dad wanted to call the cat Tiger, after the famous golfer, Tiger Woods, but there was no way I was going to have any animal named after a golfer. I mean, pleeease! I said we should give the cat a Viking name. Dad wanted to know why.

'Because he looks like one.'

'He's a cat, Trevor. How does he look like a Viking?'

'He's fierce and hairy,' I said. 'Vikings were fierce and hairy too – except the bald ones, of course. They were probably just fierce.'

Dad gazed at me for several seconds while he struggled to find the right words. His mouth moved several times but no sound came out. Eventually he gave in.

'All right. Erik it is.' Dad looked across at the cat. 'What do you think of that, Erik?'

Erik sat up, made several icky noises, stretched out his neck and head and finally coughed up a small hairball.

'Lovely,' muttered Dad. 'I don't remember the Vikings doing that.' He began to move away but Erik had other ideas and threw himself at Dad's left leg as he brushed past, sinking in his claws.

'OWW!'

Erik let go and stalked off, his tail high in the air. If he could speak he would have been saying:

'Don't mess with me, sonny. I'm Erik the Viking.' I smiled inwardly, rather proud of the name I'd just given him. I bet Erik likes it.

Funnily enough, Erik loves Streaker and her puppies. They get on really well. Erik plays with them. He lets them jump on him and chase his tail. And Erik and Streaker are great friends. They sit together for hours. It sounds mad but sometimes you'd think they were actually talking to each other.

However, none of this will stop Mum and Dad from selling the puppies. Dad put up a card in our local shop saying PUPPIES FOR SALE and he posted another one in the club house at the golf course he goes to.

(Groan groan. Golf. WHAT IS THAT ABOUT? I will tell you. It's about people wandering around all day looking for a tiny ball they've lost. The only thing they use their golf clubs for is poking about in nettles. And then, when they DO find the ball, what do they do? They hit it again, lose it again and spend the next three years in another search. And that's meant to be A GAME?)

Anyhow, a strange man came round this afternoon to take a look at the pups. I could tell he was strange the moment I saw him. He had an enormous moustache. It was truly gigantic. It looked like he had a yak hanging off the end of his nose. And his eyes were swimming about behind thick spectacles.

His name was Mr Slocumber and he loved the puppies and drooled over them. Honestly, it was disgusting, you should have heard him.

'Oh, they are so GORGEOUS! Oh, look, look, they've got PAWS!' (What did he expect to find – monster lobster pincers?)

'I love them. They are so funny. And look, look, look – this one's got FUNNY EARS!'

'They've all got ears,' I pointed out.

'I know! AREN'T THEY FUNNY?!' cried Mr Slocumber.

'All dogs have ears,' I growled.

'I know! AREN'T THEY FUNNY?!' he repeated yet again, bending over the pups.

I was just wishing the yak under his nose would stampede down his throat and suffocate him when a four-legged ginger Viking thundered across from behind a cupboard, launched himself at Mr Slocumber's rather large backside and clung there, like a small lion trying to bring down an elephant.

Mr Slocumber straightened sharply, eyes wide with alarm and his mouth hanging open in a silent scream. Erik slowly let go and backed down the poor man's leg, digging in his claws on the way. Then off he went, tail in the air, as usual.

'He's been teaching the puppies to do that,' I hinted.

'Really?' squeaked Mr Slocumber, backing away.

'They've got ALL their teeth now,' I added for extra effect. 'You'd be surprised how sharp they are for such little nippers.'

'Would I?' croaked Mr Slocumber. He had turned rather white, quite possibly through loss of blood in the leg and bottom areas. He didn't stay much longer. Victory! I felt quite proud of myself! Mind you, I hope Mum and Dad don't find out.

2. A Gorilla in Boots

Of course I do know that the pups will have to go, sooner or later. I just want to enjoy them a bit longer. I want them to be with us for Christmas. Surely that's not too much to ask? Streaker's going to miss them too when they've gone. And Erik as well, even if he is a bloodthirsty little Viking.

I reckoned Tina would enjoy my story about Mr Slocumber so I told Mum I was nipping out to see her. Mum raised her eyebrows a trifle.

'When's the wedding?'

I knew she was only teasing but it is SO ANNOYING. Tina and I have been friends for ages and because she's a girl everyone makes boyfriend and girlfriend jokes. But we are just good friends. HONESTLY.

Mind you, Tina does like getting close. Sometimes she leans against me or tries to loop her arm through mine when we're walking. When I ask her to stop she tells me I should 'chill' and be more 'tactile'.

'What does *tactile* mean?' I was suspicious.

'It means you shouldn't scream when I touch you,' she grunted.

Tina lives just round the corner and she's got this MASSIVE St Bernard called Mouse. (Ha ha.) 'Why don't we walk into the centre and see

how the Christmas decorations are going? You can tell me all about Mr Cucumber on the way.'

'Slocumber,' I corrected.

'Slocumber, Fastcumber, jumber-cumber,' she laughed.

'Tina, you are a complete twittle.'

'What is a twittle when it's at home?' she asked.

'A little twit, of course. Ta da!'

'Thank you,' Tina answered evenly. 'You can go home now if you like.'

You can see that Tina and I enjoy our little conversations.

By this time we were practically in the centre of town. The council workmen were out in force, rigging up a big Christmas tree and dangling lights from just about everything that didn't move.

Tina beamed. 'It's going to be so – twinkly,' she gushed. 'And romantic,' she added, slipping her arm through mine. I automatically flinched.

'What's the matter?' Tina asked, as innocent as

a cat with a bird in its mouth. I had just started to
try to extricate my arm when there was a brash
guffaw from behind.

'Well, if it isn't Mr and Mrs Lovey-Dovey.'

I whirled round and found myself face to face
with a gorilla in a coat, and his three Alsatians.

'Charlie Smugg,' I groaned, yanking my arm free of Tina at last. I could feel my face heating up fast. I probably looked like a boiled tomato. Charlie sniggered.

'Go on, give her a kiss,' he urged, a big grin splitting his spotty, fat face. 'There's mistletoe going up there – go on, have a Christmas snog.'

He's disgusting, Charlie – a nightmare in boots. He's fourteen and he hates Tina and me. We've been kind of locked in a war with him for ages. AND he's got those horrible dogs – THREE of them. They're all teeth, and growl and snap and slobber. You might have thought that having Mouse with us would be some protection, but Tina's St Bernard sat behind us, innocently watching the workmen ferrying bunches of mistletoe up the lamp posts.

'Get lost, Charlie,' Tina suggested. Charlie scowled and let his dogs surge at us, flashing their horrible white teeth and curling back their lips so we could see their mottled pink gums. Tina and I recoiled several paces.

'My dogs don't like it when people are rude,' snarled Charlie.

'Don't know how they live with you then,' Tina answered.

I do so wish she wouldn't talk like that – NOT TO CHARLIE SMUGG of all people. Maybe it's all right for her, being a girl. But I'm fish-food as far as Charlie's concerned, and he's the biggest shark in town. Charlie let his dogs rush us again.

'Goodbye, Charlie,' I said, as evenly as possible. I could feel my heart speeding up. He's a big lad.

'Whoa!' yelled Charlie as his Alsatians almost pulled him off his feet. Mouse sat there and watched. He might just as well have been having his nails done.

Charlie began to move off but then stopped and came back. With a smile. 'Oh yes, I knew there was something on my mind. How are those puppies of yours?'

Why should he be interested in Streaker's puppies? I wondered. He must be up to something. Charlie didn't care about anything except himself.

'They're OK.'

He nodded. 'Thought so, cos I saw that card in the shop – Puppies For Sale – and it had your surname. Now then, I think we need to talk about them pups. You're selling them, aren't you?'

'So?' I muttered.

'Well now, seems to me that we need to do a deal, cos those pups aren't exactly yours, are they?'

'No, they're Streaker's,' I answered.

'That's not what I mean,' Charlie went on, wagging a fat finger at my face. 'I remember when those pups were born and I reckon the father of those pups was one of my dogs.'

Charlie's face had turned seriously threatening by now. I knew exactly what he was talking about. Charlie's Alsatians had chased Streaker several months earlier and cornered her behind a shed. Nobody knew exactly what happened but very soon after that we found Streaker was pregnant and then the pups were born.

'So the thing is,' Charlie continued, 'I reckon that since one of my dogs was the dad I should have half the money when you sell them.' His face lit up with another smile. He looked like a shark who'd just found his midday meal and was about to swallow it. Whole. And the meal was me.

'In your dreams,' snapped Tina. 'Firstly, it was Streaker who had the pups, not your Alsatians. Secondly, you can't prove it was one of your dogs. Thirdly, you're a big bully, so get lost, again.'

Wow! Tina can be pretty feisty. I swallowed hard and wondered what Charlie would do about this. The gorilla looked around but there were lots of shoppers out and about. He licked his lips again.

'Pretty words, but it don't change anything. When those pups get sold I want my money and I'll be after you for it. It won't just be me either. I've got my dogs. They're bigger than yours and there are more of them.'

'We've got Mouse,' I boasted.

'Oh yes, the hugely evil St Bernard,' said Charlie, patting Mouse's massive head. Tina's dog immediately lay down, rolled over and displayed his belly for tickling.

'I am SO SCARED,' Charlie sniggered. 'Got to go now. Don't forget – half the money, or ALL the trouble.'

It was several minutes after Charlie had gone before my heart stopped trying to clamber out of my chest and run away to sea. Charlie meant business.

'What do we do?' I asked Tina.

'Kill him?'

'No, I mean seriously, Tina.'

'Kill him?' she repeated and shrugged. 'I don't know. What *can* we do?'

'We need a plan,' I muttered.

'Yes, that will help. Then we can hit him over the head with it. You'd better make sure it's a very big heavy plan, hopefully in the shape of a gigantic club, like cavemen used on dinosaurs, because that's what Charlie is.'

Sometimes Tina can be very annoying (and sarcastic). On the other hand, she stood up to Charlie Smugg – GULP! I would never have dared speak to him like that. She told him to get lost! Mouse wasn't much help, though. He's about as tough as a – well, about as tough as a mouse, I guess.

I was thinking all this when I suddenly had a bit of an idea. I grabbed Tina's arm and she beamed at me.

'At last! See, you like it really.' She fluttered her eyelashes.

'Tina, shut up and be serious.'

'I *was* being serious,' she grumbled.

'I've got an idea, and it's simple.'

'Of course it is, you're a boy.'

I ignored that. 'What we have to do is make sure the puppies never get sold.'

'How are we going to do that?' she asked, and I reminded her about Mr Slocumber.

'OK, so you managed to stop one person, but your parents want to sell them. You can't be there every time someone comes to look at the puppies.'

'At least we can try to delay our deaths at the hands of Charlie,' I insisted.

'Or the jaws of three Alsatians,' murmured Tina unhelpfully. She snapped her fingers. 'Got it! We tell Charlie that your parents are giving the dogs away for free. If they're given away there's no money problem.'

'Suppose he doesn't believe us? He's seen that card in the shop.'

'OK, in that case we shall have to persuade your parents not to sell them but to give them away.'

I wasn't so sure. I thought it was highly doubtful that Mum and Dad would change their minds.

'It's a matter of Life or Death, Trevor,' Tina said firmly. 'OUR lives and OUR deaths.'

I had to admit that she did have a point.

3. The Great Vanishing

I knew they wouldn't. Parents are so predictable.
Dad was wearing full golfing gear and practising
his putting in the front room when I popped the

question. He sliced the ball so hard it almost whizzed out of the window, just missing Erik the Viking as he lazed on top of the sofa. Erik flicked one ear and went back to sleep. He is one cool cat.

'GIVE the puppies AWAY?' squawked Dad. 'Are you mad?'

'Only occasionally,' I muttered. In fact I was

thinking that if anyone was mad it must be my dad, playing golf in his front room. If only he could see himself.

Mum said Christmas was an expensive time of year. 'We need that extra money from those puppies, and goodness me, they owe us enough.'

'Streaker's pups owe you money?' What had Mum been doing? Lending the pups money so they could nip down to the local sweet shop to spend it?

'Do you know how much it costs to feed three hungry puppies?' she grumbled. 'Not to mention all the jabs they've just had from the vet so they can go outside safely – which incidentally is something you can do now, since you're obviously not busy.'

This conversation was definitely not going the way it was meant to.

'It's snowing,' I argued.

'Children love snow,' Mum replied, while Dad chuckled.

'She's got you there, Trevor.'

'I don't like snow. It's cold. It's
down the back of my neck.'

Mum glanced outside. 'It's hardly
all. Stop moaning, get your coat and t.
pups for a walk. It's about time they saw the
outside world.'

'If I get a cold it'll be your fault,' I muttered.

'Out,' said Mum.

'And if I get Martian Flu or whatever and DIE
you'll be really sorry.'

'And if you don't take those pups out you won't
get any Christmas,' suggested Dad, which was
very unkind of him.

'What about my human rights?' I started.

'What? You're human? Nobody told me!'
exclaimed Dad.

'Ha ha, very funny,' I scowled. 'Just because
you're bigger than me.'

'Just because you're smaller than me,' Dad
laughed.

29

you wait until I'm grown up,' I threatened.

'Why? What will you do then?' Mum asked, arms folded and a big smile on her face.

'I'll – I'll – I'll tell you: I'll leave home!'

And you know what? THEY BOTH SIGHED WITH RELIEF. MY OWN PARENTS!

'You don't understand,' I shouted. 'If I leave home, YOU'LL HAVE TO WALK STREAKER!'

Their faces fell and they exchanged alarmed glances. Ha! I had them now!

'The boy's right,' muttered Dad.

'Disaster,' nodded Mum. 'What are we going to do?'

'Better make sure Trevor walks the dogs now while he's still with us,' Dad suggested.

'Just what I was thinking,' agreed Mum. 'The lead's hanging up by the front door, Trev. You know how to let yourself out, don't you?'

So that worked out really well for me, didn't

it? I grabbed the lead – although actually it was three mini leads on the end of one main lead – and off we went, trudging through the snow.

This was the first time the puppies had been beyond the house and the first time they had been on the triple lead. Plus, I had Streaker with me too, and she kept dancing round her children.

So what really happened was that the puppies immediately got tied up in knots. They fell over themselves and bit each other while their mum tried to sort things out by jumping in with them and making things ten times worse. It wasn't long before I came to a complete stop. I now had three puppies and one dog wrapped round my legs and I couldn't budge.

I glanced around for help and eventually a little old lady toddled into sight and took pity on me. Honestly, it was SO embarrassing.

'You give me that end to hold,' she said, 'and I'll just lift this little pup up – aren't they cute! Oh, I think he's doing a tiddle in mid-air. I'd better put him down. There. Let's move this one round instead. Can you get your big dog to stop trying to hide under my coat? No? Oh dear, I've got my foot stuck now. Can you . . . ? No, you can't move either, can you?' she sighed. 'I think we'll have to wait for help.'

Five minutes later we were still standing there,

thoroughly stuck, while the little old lady told me
about her grandson who had a tortoise that was
so big you could ride on him, but sadly he had
awful spots on his face – the grandson, not the
tortoise. I was just thinking I wanted to doze off
rather than listen to any more when a passing fire
engine saw our problem and pulled over.

Four firemen got out and it didn't take them
too long to untangle us from the leads, sniggering
all the while.

'Good thing we saw you,' said one. 'We were
on our way back to the station from a job.'

'Thank you, officer,' beamed the old lady. 'You are most kind. I don't suppose you're going past the shops, are you? Maybe you could give me a lift.' And off she went with the firemen. The last I heard from her she was starting to tell them about her grandson's spots. As for me, I headed straight for the park and a bit of peace and quiet – or so I hoped. At least the pups weren't too manic.

There wasn't much snow, only a centimetre or so, but it had turned the park into a gigantic, clean bed sheet. The dogs and I had great fun mucking it up by putting funny paw prints all over the place.

I freed the pups from their little leads and off they went, bopping and bouncing, flopping in the snow and generally being terribly cute. They were so funny. They kept slipping and falling over and trying to nip each other on the bum or the ear.

Streaker loves a bit of snow and she went tearing off in about ten different directions at once. As soon as she sees anything she thinks might be remotely interesting she's away. It might be another dog or it might simply be a tiny bit of twig. She'll spend ages nudging it with her nose, trying to toss it into the air. (The twig, not the other dog.)

It was while Streaker was doing one of her vanishing acts that it happened. The pups decided to disappear too. All three of them suddenly went charging off into the nearby bushes. I guessed they'd probably seen some poor rabbit, though if they were anything like their mother the rabbit was almost certainly imaginary. Streaker is always chasing rabbits that don't exist except in her head.

I stood there at the edge of the park, idly kicking at the snow and waiting for the pups to return, not to mention Streaker. Eventually I spotted a dark dot on the far horizon. It was an incoming four-legged missile, getting bigger and bigger, hurtling towards me, homing in on its target – typical Streaker. She arrived at full speed, knocking me into the snow. She'd obviously decided my face was filthy because she launched a major clean-up operation with her tongue.

At last she stopped, sat back on her haunches and looked around expectantly. The pups hadn't returned. I sat up and scanned the park too. No sign of them, which was odd. I got to my feet and Streaker followed me to the bushes. We peered between the branches and I called out, but there was only silence. I couldn't even hear them crashing about anywhere. It's astonishing

how silent silence can be when you're really listening, not to mention eerie.

Streaker had her nose to the ground and was sniff sniff sniffing. She ran round behind the bushes and I followed. No puppies. The only things to be seen were an awful lot of puppy paw prints. AND ONE SET OF GREAT BIG HUMAN FOOTPRINTS. The puppies had vanished. In fact they had been stolen – DOGNAPPED!

4. The Hunt Begins

Streaker stood there, trying to look intelligent. This is very difficult to achieve when you have a large floppy tongue dangling from your front end and a windscreen-wiper tail stuck on your back.

'Follow the scent,' I urged. Streaker bounced round me, all bright eyes and no brain. 'No, not jumping. We're on a SEARCH, Streaker. We are LOOK-ING. Find your puppies! We're not doing jumping today. You can do that when you find the dog thief and then you can jump on them as much as you like.'

Streaker began barking, which was a great help, and then carried on dancing round me. I might just as well have taken her to a disco.

It was no use. The puppies had gone. It was almost as if they'd been beamed up into a

passing UFO by dog-loving aliens on their way
to Planet Crufts. At least I hoped they loved dogs.
I followed the footprints to the edge of the park,
over the low wall and on to the footpath. There
the prints had been trodden into a mush by lots
of other feet. The trail was dead, which was just
about how I felt myself.

I went home trailing a lead with no puppies on
the end of it. Streaker followed slowly. She kept
looking behind her in case the pups suddenly
appeared, chasing happily after her as they

usually did. I had to tell Mum and Dad. What else could I do? Dad muttered something about it being just his luck and why couldn't the robber have stolen Streaker instead? I knew he was joking, but it was unkind.

Dad insisted we all trudged back to the park and searched again but I knew it was useless long before we even got there. Dad was getting more and more cross and muttering all the awful things he'd like to do to the puppy thief.

'I'll make them eat dog food for the rest of their lives,' he seethed. 'I'll put them on a lead and drag them to the vet and get the vet to give them the biggest injection EVER with the biggest needle EVER, right into their BUM.'

'Dad!'

When we got home everyone was in a bad mood, including me. I went to my room, threw myself on my bed and wondered what to do next.

Streaker came up and did the same. We both lay there, staring at the ceiling, with Streaker's

legs poking up in the air like cocktail sticks in a
big sausage. She looked completely stupid, but
then she always does. She's daft and I love her.
And I love her pups too and they'd just been
stolen.

Where were they? What was happening to them? They could be in danger. Maybe they weren't being fed properly, or not fed at all. Maybe some really nasty person wanted to make them into slippers or earmuffs, finger-warmers, nose-warmers!

My brain was torturing me with awful thoughts. I didn't even know if there was such a thing as a nose-warmer. I had to do something, so I thought I'd start by going to see Tina. She often has good ideas. Mind you, she often has crazy ones too, but at least it was someone to talk to.

'Stolen!' she cried. 'Who took them?'

'Your guess is as good as mine,' I answered wearily. 'It could have been anyone, except that the footprints were big – I'm sure it was a man.'

'Why not a woman?'

'Women's feet aren't as big as men's,' I replied.

'Huh. You haven't met my aunt, have you? She wears canal boats on *her* feet.'

'All right, but most likely it was a man,' I insisted.

'Why would anyone want to steal puppies?' Tina asked.

'Christmas? They could give them as a present. Maybe they want to sell them. Does it matter? We've got to get them back. They could be in danger.'

Tina chewed her lip for a moment. 'Well, at least Charlie Smugg can't bother us for that money any more. If they've been stolen they can't be sold.'

I knew Tina was trying to be helpful but even that didn't cheer me up. I wanted the pups back in the house. 'We've got to find them,' I repeated.

'We need to investigate,' Tina declared. 'We'll start at the scene of the crime, and we'll take Mouse with us.'

'What good will he be?'

'St Bernards are trained to track down people,' Tina explained.

'I know, but I thought they had to be buried in avalanches first of all so the dogs can dig them out.'

Tina pointed out of the window. 'It's been snowing,' she said cheerfully.

'Tina, we don't get avalanches in the park. It's very flat.'

Tina clutched both my shoulders and shook me. 'Do you want to find those pups or not?'

'OK, OK. I'm coming.'

We went to the park for my third visit, dragging Mouse along with us. With Streaker it's the other way round. You don't take her anywhere – she takes you, at high speed. Mouse is quite the opposite. It's like dragging a gigantic pudding behind you.

'Right. This is where it happened,' I told Tina. 'Look, you can still see the puppies' paw marks, and mine – and those are the big footprints I told you about.'

Tina bent over the prints then straightened,

gazed around and fixed me with a suspicious eye.
'You didn't see anyone behind the bushes?'

'No, officer.'

'And what were you doing when all this happened?' she asked, making notes in a little book.

'I was either watching Streaker or being given a bath by her.'

'Why did she bath you?' Tina quizzed.

'She thought I had a filthy face.'

'Is that your alibi?' Tina demanded severely.

'Yes, and if you'll pardon me for saying, officer, I'm not likely to steal my own puppies, am I?'

Tina gave a stiff nod and snapped shut her notebook. 'Good point. All right, I shan't arrest you this time, but watch your step. Aha!' She suddenly plunged one hand into the bushes and pulled out a small scrap of dark navy cloth.

'Look! A scrap of cloth. I think it comes from clothing worn by the criminal. All we have to do is match this to their coat.' Tina smiled triumphantly.

'Tina, that scrap of cloth might have been there for ages. We don't know it comes from the criminal's coat and, besides, how many people have dark coats? Just about everyone, that's how many.'

Tina pocketed the scrap and shrugged. 'Maybe, but we can at least keep an eye out for someone with a torn jacket. Let's follow the footprints.' She bent over the tracks and slowly traced them to the low wall at the edge of the park. She stared at the mess of prints on the far side of the wall.

'Mmm,' she muttered. 'Interesting. It's difficult to say for sure, but I think the dognapper turned right when he left the park, which means he didn't go into the centre of town. That's important.'

I closed my eyes for a weary second and spoke slowly. 'Yes, very important. If he didn't go into town all we have to do now is search THE REST OF THE WORLD.'

'Trevor, you are being very difficult this morning,' Tina grumbled.

'I'm having a difficult day. Streaker's puppies have been stolen.'

Tina took hold of my right hand in both of hers. I could feel the warmth through her gloves. She looked straight into my eyes. 'We are going to find them,' she said with great sincerity.

She had obviously stopped pretending to be a policewoman and was now a trauma counsellor.

I wanted to believe her. Even more, I wanted her to stop holding my hand. It was embarrassing. I pulled it away and stuffed both hands firmly into my pockets. Tina gave a little smile.

'One day –' she began, but didn't finish.

'One day what?' I asked.

'Oh, nothing. I think we've seen enough. Burping botties! Isn't that Charlie Smugg walking towards us?'

It *was* Charlie, and he'd spotted us. It was too late to escape. At least he didn't have his wretched Alsatians with him.

'Afternoon, lovebirds,' he greeted us, flashing his broken-toothed smile. 'How's it going? Got my money yet?'

I was going to enjoy telling Charlie the next bit. 'No, we haven't and you won't ever get it either, because we no longer have the pups. They've been stolen.'

'Stolen! Never!' Charlie scowled and poked
my chest with a fat finger. 'How do I know you're
telling the truth?'

'Check my house,' I offered and told him what
had happened in the park.

'Who'd want to do something like that?'
Charlie mused.

'Somebody who reckons they'd make a good
Christmas present,' Tina suggested.

'Yeah, suppose.' Charlie was frowning harder and harder. Evidently he was trying to piece together some thought that had occurred deep inside his tiny brain.

'Thing is,' he began, 'those pups are still half mine. Now, I didn't lose those pups, you did, and that's your responsibility, so the way I see it is like you still owe me half the money.'

'Charlie!' Tina and I chorused in disbelief.

Our horror put an even bigger smile on Charlie's face. 'Oh yeah,' he nodded. 'You still owe me all right. I want to see that money, before Christmas, or there'll be trouble. Big trouble. Bye now. Have a nice day.'

Tina and I watched in stunned silence as Charlie went clumping off in his big boots and vanished round the corner.

5. Criminals!

Streaker was pounding round the house, diving under tables, snuffling behind chairs and burrowing beneath beds. She was on a frantic puppy hunt. She tried to climb up the chimney at one point. How do I know? Because she appeared in the kitchen surrounded by a large cloud of soot. She waved her tail frantically, which only spread the filth further.

Mum took one look at her and hurried to the front room, following the very noticeable trail of black paw prints. 'That dog! (*Cough!*) That wretched (*cough cough*) pesky dog!'

I crept to the door. Soot was still billowing from the fireplace. The room had been hit by a soot avalanche. It was everywhere, and so were Streaker's paw marks – on the furniture,

walls, cushions and carpet. I wouldn't have been
surprised to see a set of them marching across
the ceiling. The front room was a major disaster
area, and Mum was threatening an even more
major explosion over the dog.

I decided that Streaker and I had better go

and hide somewhere safe until the soot storm
blew over. What we really needed was a nuclear
bunker nearby where we could lock ourselves
away, but since there wasn't one we nipped
round to Tina's.

Her mother opened the door, took one look at

the soot-caked Streaker and politely told us to use the side gate into the garden. 'Keep her on the lead and I'll hose her down,' she ordered.

It was a good idea – a neat, simple idea. It should have worked, but it didn't. Why not? Because it involved Streaker. When Tina's mum turned on the hose and the jet of water hit Streaker she gave a wild yelp. Her eyes practically

popped out of her head. She leaped into my arms for shelter and immediately scrabbled about like crazy, generally making sure that I had as much wet soot as possible plastering me from top to bottom. Finally she plopped back down and gave herself a good shake, just to finish things off. Another wave of soggy soot hit me like a tsunami.

'This is fun,' I said grimly.

Tina's mother stood with the hose dangling from one hand. 'Oh dear,' she murmured. 'That didn't quite work out as I expected. Maybe the water was a bit cold.'

'It's freezing!' I cried. I could swear Tina's mother was trying not to laugh. One thing was certain, Tina thought it hilarious. She was leaning out of her bedroom window and howling with glee.

'You look so funny, Trev!'

'Thank you.'

'You're such a gong!'

'Thank you,' I repeated, even more coldly.

Tina's mother threw me a towel. 'Dry yourself off and then do the dog.' She studied my soot-suit with a grimace. 'I can't let either of you in like that, either.'

'Oh, great,' I muttered. 'We'll freeze out here.'

'I'll come down to you,' said Tina and a few moments later she emerged from the house with an extra towel and began to mop Streaker. I told her about Streaker's chimney investigation while I dried myself. Tina leaped to the dog's defence.

'Streaker's bound to miss her pups,' Tina sighed. 'Of course she's going to look for them.'

'UP THE CHIMNEY?' I raised my eyebrows. 'Where will she search next? Down the toilet?'

Tina shrugged. 'She is only a dog. You can't expect her to think like a human.'

'You can't expect her to think, full stop,' I grunted, and to prove what I had just said Streaker chose that moment to make a single, graceful leap over the side gate, out to the front and she was gone.

'Uh-oh, here we go again,' I groaned. 'Streaker's on the trail. Come on, hurry. Maybe she's got a hot scent.'

We reached the road just in time to see Streaker skid round the corner at the far end. 'She's heading for town. Run! Can't you go any faster?'

'Yes,' said Tina, breezing past me. I should have remembered she'd won the hundred-metre sprint on Sports Day. Show-off. Mind you, I was running in wet jeans and squelchy shoes that had more soot in them than feet. Lovely.

We raced towards the centre of town – at least, Tina raced, I just kind of squidged at speed. I was thinking, how many times have I done this before – gone chasing after my hundred-mile-an-hour dog? Hundreds of times, that's how many.

We slowed down as we reached the main square. We had to because it was crowded with shoppers and the council were still putting up Christmas decorations. Piles of cables and lights lay beside plastic Father Christmases, angels, snowmen and elves, all laid out ready to go up. Prickly heaps of holly and mistletoe were sprinkled here and there, waiting to be used. And somewhere among all that was Streaker.

Funnily enough (though it wasn't funny at the time), it was quite easy to spot her. The first sign we got was a loud, alarmed yell.

'HELP!'

We gazed in the direction of the shout just in time to see a long ladder go crashing to the ground. A workman clung with one hand to the top of a lamp post, legs dangling helplessly. His free hand was clutching a fat, plastic Santa by the foot, but not for long. A moment later he let go and Father Christmas plunged head first to the ground and smashed to bits.

The crowd gasped with horror.

'HELP!!' cried the workman again and several people rushed to his aid, propping up the ladder for him. Streaker eyed the gathering crowd with an innocent look on her face that said it all – *Ladder? What ladder? Who? Me?*

As the crowd approached she decided to scarper, double quick, but by this time she had managed to get a strand of lights tangled round her back legs. The workmen saw this as a chance to grab her. They quickly dropped the ladder and closed on Streaker, shouting at her and arguing with each other over how best to catch her. The dangling man went on dangling (and yelling).

'HELP!'

'Go round the other side and head her off!'

'Wave a bone at her!'

'Where am I going to find a bone, you idiot?'

'Flap your coat. It scares them.'

'Flap your own coat. Just go round the other side, will you?'

'HELLLPPPPPP!'

'We need a bone!'

'You need a brain.'

'You saying I'm stupid?'

Heaven knows how long this would have gone on for when the situation took a turn for the worse. Charlie Smugg appeared, and he wasn't alone. He had his three Alsatians, straining at the leash. An unpleasant smile crept on to his face as he took in the situation and spotted Streaker, trapped in the Christmas cables. Charlie planted his legs wide, grinned and let loose his howling pack.

The Alsatians bounded away like wolves just coming off a starvation diet, their long legs swallowing the ground between them and their prey. Their gnashing jaws were flecked with frothy spit. I could see the panic in Streaker's eyes as they hurtled towards her. Normally she could have outrun them, but she was still struggling, entangled in at least three different sets of Christmas lights.

She made a dash to escape but it was hard
work with all those bulbs following behind,
bouncing and bursting on the road. But now
the workmen and Charlie's Alsatians also found
themselves getting tangled up in endless coils of
cable too.

It began to look as if they were all fighting some gigantic monster from the depths of the sea as they struggled with snaking coils of coloured bulbs, not to mention the odd holly branch and umpteen plastic elves and snowmen. The shouts grew louder as more people were drawn into battle. And the more people tried to help, the worse the situation became.

DEE DOO DEE DOO DEE DOO!

Everyone was drowned out by the arrival of a police car. It came swooping into the square and was almost brought to a halt by the wriggling wire monster, not to mention the boggle-eyed snowmen, Santas and fairies that kept popping up from time to time.

Instead of stopping the car and getting out, the driver decided that the best way to deal with the problem was to make his siren wail even louder.

DEE DOO DEE DOO!!!!

It was Sergeant Smugg, of course, Charlie's dad. The police car inched forward, deafening the entire town, scrunching over bulbs, cables and the shattered fragments of exploding elves and fairies. Finally the car stopped and out stepped Sergeant Smugg, hitching up his trousers like some gun-slinging sheriff. He couldn't see what was going on so he climbed on to the bonnet of his car, megaphone in hand.

'Who started this riot?' bellowed Sergeant Smugg, while his megaphone went into feed-back mode and delivered such an ear-splitting screech it knocked the sergeant clean off his feet.

He landed smack on his butt on the bonnet of his car and immediately slid straight off and on to the ground. He lay there for a second and then struggled back to his feet.

'I repeat: who started this riot?'

'WILL SOMEBODY *PLEEEASE* HELP ME?!' pleaded the workman who was STILL dangling from the lamp post.

For a second or two there was no answer. Everyone looked around, wondering what to do, their eyes flicking from the dangling workman to the town sheriff. They knew it wasn't exactly a riot, but how *had* it all started? Nobody seemed to be sure. At least, nobody seemed sure until Charlie Smugg spoke up.

'It was that pesky dog, Streaker,' he shouted at his dad. 'It was Streaker and Trevor and that girlfriend of his.'

There was a short silence and then everyone took up the cry. 'Yes! It was Streaker and Trevor and his girlfriend. There they are!'

We suddenly found a hundred fingers pointing at us, while on the other side of the square the dangling workman finally let go. And that was how Tina, Streaker and I came to be in the police station, almost under arrest. (And the workman came to be in hospital, under sedation.)

6. Suspicious Behaviour

Tina was outraged. 'Charlie doesn't know what happened. He wasn't even there when it started! You can't keep us here. It's against the law.'

'That's not the case, young lady,' smirked Sergeant Smugg. 'Upholding the law is down to the police, and in this town that means me. I am the police and starting a riot is a serious offence.'

'We didn't start a riot,' I tried to explain. 'And if Charlie hadn't let his dogs loose none of this would have happened.'

'You can't wriggle out of it by blaming my son,

son,' snorted the sergeant, and he shook his head because what he'd said didn't sound right at all. He pulled a face and squinted at me, hard. 'Don't you *ever* bath?' he asked.

Before I could open my mouth Tina butted in. 'He's on his way to a fancy dress party,' she said with a completely straight face. 'He's going as his own shadow. I think that's really clever, don't you?'

At that moment Dad arrived to save us, closely followed by Tina's mother. Dad did not look happy.

'How many times have I had to collect you from this police station, Trevor? No, don't even tell me. And, of course, it wasn't your fault, was it, or Streaker's?'

'Honestly, Dad, it wasn't.'

'It never is, is it?' muttered Sergeant Smugg, rather sarcastically.

Dad ignored him. He had suddenly become aware of my state of darkness. 'What *have* you been doing?' he gasped.

'He's in fancy dress,' explained Sergeant Smugg. 'He's going as his own shadow. Quite clever, really,' he grunted.

'Don't be ridiculous,' snapped Dad. 'Are you charging anyone here with an offence?'

Sergeant Smugg gave an unpleasant smile and began counting on his fingers. 'Let me see: damaging council property, causing an affray, inflicting bodily harm, preventing the progress of a police vehicle, causing a riot –' Sergeant Smugg paused for effect, leaned across his desk and finished off – 'AND THAT'S JUST THE DOG.'

Streaker gave a short 'woof' and shook a bit

more soot off her coat. The sergeant took several steps away from her. 'As for these two, you can get put in prison for rioting, you know.'

Tina's mother stepped forward. 'Officer, I am going to take these two children home, along with the dog, because neither dogs nor children go to prison. You carry on with your investigation and if you want to get in touch you know where we shall be. Goodbye, Sergeant.'

Tina's mother ushered us outside.

'Pompous twit,' muttered Dad. 'So what *did* happen then?'

Tina and I took it in turns to explain.

'I can easily believe that. Charlie Smugg is always causing trouble,' said Tina's mother. 'I used to teach him, you know, when he was about four or five. He was a troublemaker then and he hasn't changed. His parents never listened. It was always someone else's fault.' She gave a little sigh. 'What's all this I hear about missing puppies?'

So then we had to tell the story of the pups.

Tina's mother asked us if we'd come across any clues.

'All we know is that they were stolen from the park and we don't think the robber brought them into town. The prints in the snow seemed to show that he or she went in the opposite direction,' explained Tina.

'Oh, out towards the golf course?' queried Dad.

'Yes.'

'They could be anywhere by now,' Dad added unhelpfully.

Tina's mother gave a little frown. 'If you had stolen some puppies, where would you hide them?'

'I'd take them home,' said Tina.

'I wouldn't steal them in the first place,' I said, polishing my halo. 'But if I had, I guess I'd take them somewhere isolated. Puppies bark so I wouldn't want anyone to hear them.'

Tina smiled. 'You'd make a great policeman. I like a man in uniform.'

That was enough to put me off being a policeman forever! Anyway, I'm going to be an animal trainer and I shall train animals not to go running off and get tangled up in miles of cable and light bulbs. I shall train them to do USEFUL things like finding people buried by avalanches in parks and rescuing workmen dangling from lamp posts, not to mention tracking down MISSING PUPPIES.

By this time we'd reached our house. Tina's mum came in for a cup of coffee and Tina waited while I nipped upstairs for a quick wash and change. Erik the Viking was on my bed. He took one look at me, his hair stood on end and in a flash he vanished beneath the bed. Oh well, it was good to know he was scared of *something*.

I took my dirty clothes downstairs and handed them to Mum for washing. Mum stared at the horrible heap spilling from her hands.

'Thank you, Trevor. It must be Christmas. You could have wrapped them up for me.' She glanced at Tina's mother and rolled her eyes. 'Boys,' she muttered.

'Girls aren't any better,' laughed Tina's mum. She turned to us. 'So where are you two detectives going to begin your investigation?'

'The golf course,' Tina said. 'The footprints went in that direction and it's isolated.'

'It's also HUGE,' I groaned.

'Got to start somewhere,' said Tina. 'Come on.'

Why is it I always seem to end up doing what Tina says? We headed for the golf course. It's a private club so we couldn't just wander about. Besides, if you've ever been on a golf course you'll know how picky golfers get.

Don't stand there! Keep off the grass! Keep off the path! Keep off the entire world! Get out of the way! Make way! Golfer coming through and I'm terribly important!

So Tina and I soon found ourselves sneaking about the course, and creeping from the cover of one bush to another. It was pretty exciting, especially as we realized that the little sheds we came across from time to time would make ideal hiding places.

We were about halfway round the course when we saw Charlie Smugg in the distance, walking and talking with someone. I chuckled. It was Sharon Blenkinsop. HIS GIRLFRIEND!

Of course, if you asked Charlie if he had a girlfriend he would deny it completely. After all, he's always making fun of people he reckons *do* have girlfriends – like me, for example. (Although I must remind you that Tina is NOT MY GIRLFRIEND.) But Tina and I once caught Charlie and Sharon HOLDING HANDS! It was brilliant! They were SO embarrassed. And now, here they were again, wandering round the golf greens with each other.

'How come those two can wander around as they please and we can't?' Tina demanded.

'Because Charlie's dad is a member of the golf club,' I answered.

'So is your dad.'

'I know. But my dad isn't a policeman and my dad's boss isn't chairman of the golf club either.'

'That stinks,' Tina muttered, and I couldn't have agreed more.

Tina and I crept as close as we could. I was disappointed to discover that they weren't holding hands, just talking. In fact, Charlie was on his mobile.

'Yeah,' he said. 'Make it Saturday. Have you got the money? Good.' Charlie listened closely for a few seconds. 'Of course they're all right. Been well looked after. Yeah. Alsatians. Pedigree? Oh yeah. OK. See you Saturday, five o'clock.'

Charlie snapped his mobile shut and grinned at Sharon. 'It's a deal,' he said. 'Fantastic.' And he draped one arm round SHARON'S SHOULDERS! Tina clutched at my arm so hard I squeaked.

Charlie spun round and it felt as though his eyes looked straight at me. 'What was that?' he demanded.

'Charlie,' moaned Sharon, 'come on. I'm getting cold.'

'Must have been a squirrel or something,' Charlie muttered. 'I hate squirrels. Tree-rats, that's what I call 'em.' He turned his attention back to his girlfriend. 'I'll give you a cuddle,' he said and winked. 'That will warm you up.'

I whispered to Tina. 'Pass me a bucket. I want to be sick.'

'There's no hope,' Tina sighed.

'No hope of what?' I asked.

'Romance is not a word you understand, is it, Trevor?'

If you ask me, Tina can be very strange
sometimes.

We waited in hushed excitement while Charlie
and Sharon wandered out of sight and earshot
before we climbed out of our bush. When Charlie
was on the phone, was he talking about the
puppies? It sounded like it.

'Except he said Alsatians,' Tina pointed out.
'Why did he say that?'

'Maybe because he reckons one of his Alsatians
is the father so he could be trying to pass the pups
off as Alsatians too. Whatever he's doing, it's going
to happen on Saturday at five.'

'That's when the big switch-on takes place,'
Tina said. 'All the Christmas lights are going on.'

'I'm sure he's got those pups,' I growled. 'And
he's planning to sell them himself. We've got to
stop him.'

'How? We don't even know for sure that Charlie
does have the puppies and even if he does, where
is he keeping them? It's Saturday tomorrow,

which only gives us the rest of today and half of tomorrow to find them before Charlie hands them over – if he's got them.'

'Charlie is the only suspect we've got,' I said bluntly. 'And everything fits.'

'Sure, but those pups could be hidden anywhere, absolutely anywhere.'

Tina and I stood in the middle of the golf course surrounded by wide open spaces. It felt as if we would have to search the entire world. We were startled by a loud yell. A small white ball landed with a thud nearby and rolled towards my feet.

'Oi! You kids! Buzz off! This is a golf course! Go on, clear off!'

Tina was outraged. 'That could have hit us!' she seethed.

I grabbed the ball and chucked it towards the golfer as hard as I could. 'Here's your ball back!' I yelled.

And then we ran for it, almost as fast as Streaker.

7. And the Contents of the Shed Were . . .

I had a brainwave in the night. In fact my brainwave was trotting about my bedroom sniffing all the clothes on my floor – shoes (yuck!), socks (YUCK!!), pants (YUCK YUCK YUCK!!!).

I was watching Streaker and wondering *why* dogs love sniffing things so much. Streaker will sniff anything – bushes, clothes, lamp posts, her friends' bottoms, her enemies' bottoms, Erik the Viking's bottom (much to his disgust), ANY bottom. Mouse is just the same as Streaker. Basically, dogs like smelling pongy things. I mean, you never see dogs sniffing roses and rolling their eyes with pleasure. (Which is what Tina's mum does, apparently.)

Anyhow, my brainwave. Tina and I had already made a half-hearted attempt to get Mouse following the scent of the pups but we'd given up when the prints ran out. Maybe we should give it another go, with TWO dogs, using the PUPPIES' SCENT! It was great. I smiled to myself, turned over and went back to sleep. Problem solved.

Did I say problem solved? I wish. When I woke in the morning it seemed different. Streaker and Mouse did not exactly have a brilliant track record for finding things. In fact they didn't have a track record for anything except possibly getting into trouble, not to mention getting Tina and myself into trouble at the same time.

I told Mum and Dad what I was planning. I'd like to say that they were impressed, but they weren't. They could see the pitfalls immediately and Mum summed it up in one word.

'Streaker?' she repeated. I nodded. Mum crossed herself. Dad drew a finger across his throat.

'You're not being very supportive,' I grumbled.

'I'm sorry, Trevor,' Dad explained, 'but I think it was only yesterday that I had to rescue the pair of you from prison on account of that dog.'

'Yes, but –'

'It wasn't Streaker's fault!' Mum and Dad chorused.

'Yes, but –'

'It's never Streaker's fault,' Dad interrupted.

'Well, it isn't,' I said stubbornly.

'It's just that she's always there,' Mum pointed out.

I got to my feet. 'You don't care what happens to those puppies, do you? They could be sold into child slavery for all you care.'

'I think you'd have to make that puppy slavery

for it to work as an idea,' Dad chuckled.

'It's not funny!' I yelled. 'Nothing with Charlie Smugg in it is funny. You two can sit here and twiddle your thumbs but Tina and I are going out there with Streaker and Mouse and we are going to find those pups and bring them home, SO THERE!' I rushed out, my face burning hot, slamming the door behind me.

'OWWWWW!!'

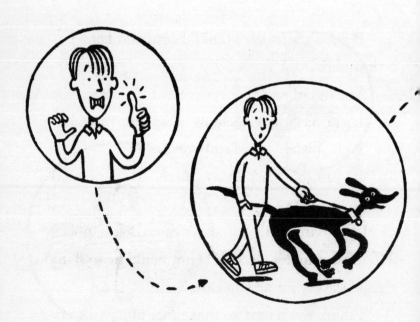

'What's up now?' asked Mum, rushing over.

'Trapped my thumb in the door when I shut it,'
I hissed. 'Leave me alone.'

I pulled away from her and set off for Tina's.
Five minutes later I turned round and went back
because I'd left without Streaker. Two minutes
after that I went back because I'd forgotten my
coat. Four minutes after that I went back because
I needed the blankets the puppies used to sleep on.

Eventually, somehow, I managed to reach Tina's and told her the whole sorry saga. She held my hand to inspect my throbbing thumb. It had turned deep red, which was actually a relief since I had thought it was falling right off. At least it was still there to be seen.

'You poor thing.' Tina said this with such sympathy I thought she was going to kiss it better. I hastily tried to pull away from her, but she tightened her grip. 'I'll get some cream.'

'Why?'

'My mum always puts special cream on bruises. It will help.'

I nodded and Tina disappeared. About a minute later she reappeared with the cream behind her back. 'Will it sting?' I asked.

'You are such a baby. Hold out your thumb.'

I closed my eyes. I hate things like scratches and bruises. There was a splurty noise and I felt something cold on my thumb. I opened my eyes. A spiral blob of whirly cream sat on top of my scarlet thumb, making it look like a miniature strawberry ice-cream cone. It was totally ridiculous.

'You said it was special cream!' I grinned. 'This is for puddings.'

'I know,' she chuckled. 'But you have to admit that makes it a VERY special cream to put on bruises.'

By this time I was laughing so much I had tears in my eyes. Tina was relieved. 'See,' she said, 'I said it would make you feel better.' That set us off laughing again.

'You are such a twit,' I told her.

'Wow, I've been promoted. Just a while back ago you told me I was only a twittle, and now I'm a proper, fully grown twit. Thank you, thank you.'

There was no more time to lose. Tina shoved a camera into her shoulder bag. 'To record any evidence,' she said and I nodded, impressed. Tina was smart.

We grabbed the dogs and the blankets and set off. The park trail had probably gone cold but we had to pick somewhere to make our start, so that was where we went. I pulled the puppies' blankets from the bag and held one to Streaker's nose while Tina did the same with Mouse.

We had decided to keep both dogs on leads, even though we knew we would both have our

arms pulled out of their sockets. (Tina's from trying to pull Mouse along behind her, and mine from trying to stop Streaker from taking off and reaching the next galaxy.)

Streaker quickly decided that I wanted to play blanket tug-of-war with her. She grabbed the other end with her teeth and began growling, snarling and pulling like fury until eventually I

gave up and just let go. She sat down heavily and looked at me with disappointed surprise.

Tina was having more success with Mouse. He sniffed the blankets carefully and then sat there, wrinkling his nose and smacking his lips as if he was tasting top-notch nosh. Finally he got to his feet and plodded off.

I tried to follow but Streaker was still sitting on her haunches and wouldn't budge. I ended up towing her along like a statue until she at last got to her feet and trotted beside me. I could have sworn she winked at me at that moment.

Mouse led us to the golf course, which wasn't much of a surprise. It was somewhere I didn't really want to go back to, if only because of the angry golfers we had run into the previous day.

It was hard to keep the dogs hidden as we were pulled across several greens. Mouse made a bee-line (or should that be a dog-line?) for wherever the scent was leading him. Fortunately there were very few golfers mad enough to want to play that morning, and finally we spotted a small shed.

Mouse headed straight for it. Streaker perked up too. She began straining at her lead and generally looking excited. My heart began to thump. I felt we were really on to something. Tina and I exchanged excited glances. This could be where the pups were being held.

As we closed in on the hut I heard voices. I was on instant alert and put a finger to my lips to signal silence, while desperately hoping that neither of the dogs would start barking.

The hut didn't have any windows so we couldn't see who was inside and we couldn't hear the voices clearly either. There was no way of telling what they were saying. I signalled to Tina that we should back away so we could figure out a plan.

'There are two of them,' I whispered.

'I couldn't hear any puppies,' Tina murmured.

'Neither could I.'

'What are we going to do?' she asked.

'We shall have to go in there.'

Tina's face was white. 'Are you sure? Won't that be dangerous?'

'We need to catch them red-handed,' I said. 'Otherwise we can't prove anything. Plus, we've got the dogs with us.'

'So what are we going to do?' she repeated.

'We burst in.'

'Then what?'

I looked at Tina. I looked at the sky. I looked at the ground. I didn't know the answer. 'I guess it depends on what they do.'

'What do you think they'll do?' asked Tina.

Honestly! Girls – they do go on. How was I supposed to know?

'We deal with the situation as it arises,' I hissed.

'What does that mean?'

'Tina! Let's just get on with it. I'll count to three. On three, you open the door and I'll rush in and confront them. If anything happens you'll be a witness. Whoever is in there can't take on both of us.'

'Right. I'll try to take a photo too.'

We moved back to the hut and prepared in silence. I mouthed the countdown.

'One – two – THREE!'

Tina yanked the door open and I rushed into the dark hut. FLASH-FLASH! The camera went off and the whole scene was brilliantly lit for a second. And there they were – Charlie Smugg and Sharon Blenkinsop – SNOGGING.

8. Back on the Trail

I immediately rushed out again, yelling at Tina.
'Run!'

Angry shouts followed as we fled. 'I'll get you!'
Charlie bellowed. 'You won't get away with this.
I'm coming after you!' He made a lunge
towards the door, knocked over a stack of golf
clubs and immediately tripped over them. He

fell to the floor, arms and legs flailing, managing to knock over two more stacks. They clattered on to him as he struggled to his feet.

'Charlie,' wailed Sharon. 'Come back here! I love you, Charlie. I'll give you another bit of chocolate.'

Charlie wasn't impressed. 'Be quiet, you daft octopus.'

The last thing we heard was Sharon giggling. 'Charlie, darling! You don't really think I'm an octopus, do you?'

We ran and ran, howling with laughter until we found ourselves at the far end of the golf course. Streaker thought it was a great game. She flew along beside us, ears bouncing while she looked up at me happily and barked her head off. Mouse lolloped along behind with his big shaggy coat flouncing about. He looked like some giant alien blob from Mars on a cheese hunt.

When we ran out of golf greens we stopped, panting and chuckling at the same time, which is pretty difficult, I can tell you. I looked back up the course. There was no sign of Charlie or Sharon.

'We're safe,' grinned Tina.

'For the time being,' I said, nodding.

'*I love you, Charlie darling!*' mimicked Tina and we started laughing again.

'She's an octopus,' I added.

'Well, he's a gorilla, so they're well matched,' said Tina. 'Did you see if the pups were there?'

I shook my head. 'You blinded me with the flash.'

'Sorreee.' Tina fiddled with the back of her camera. 'Hmm. Doesn't look like it.' She showed me the little screen and the picture she had just taken. There were the two lovebirds, Charlie and Sharon, caught forever in full snog-mode. But there were no pups.

'Maybe Charlie had been keeping them there but he's moved them somewhere else for the handover later today,' I suggested.

'That's not much help,' sniffed Tina, still

studying the photo. 'Do you think we can sell this pic to the newspapers?'

'That'd be fantastic. Charlie would be SO embarrassed. But he would also probably kill us.'

Tina shrugged. 'He's going to kill us anyway. He's probably waiting up there to ambush us on our way home.'

'We'll go back the long way. Come on.'

We set off round the far edge of the golf course. There was a footpath I knew which led to a scattering of houses, some old lock-up garages and then came out near Tina's road.

Tina glanced at her watch. 'We've got six hours left before Charlie hands over those pups.'

'I know, and we still don't know for sure that he's actually got them or where the handover will take place.'

'Thing is, everyone will be in town to watch the big light-up this evening,' said Tina. 'Everywhere else will be completely quiet. Charlie could go anywhere and nobody would notice.'

I was silent. I'd already worked this out and it was bothering me, a lot. We carried on making our way towards home, keeping a sharp eye out for Charlie and any Alsatians he might have decided to bring along for fun and games.

The footpath carried us through the block of lock-up garages. Two or three seemed to be in use but most of them had had their doors ripped off and covered in graffiti. It didn't feel like a nice place to be and I wasn't exactly surprised when the dogs began playing up.

Both of them started tugging hard on their leads. Streaker was so eager her front paws were right off the ground.

'What's up with them?' Tina asked. 'Mouse, will you behave?'

The St Bernard had his nose almost buried in the ground as he snuffled along. My heart gave a tiny leap. I told myself not to get excited and let slip Streaker's lead. She went tearing off like a rocket, heading straight for one of the lock-ups. She didn't even bother to slow down or stop, but hurled herself at the metal door, scratching it wildly and barking, barking, barking.

Tina and I exchanged one amazed glance and ran across to the locked garage. Inside we could hear little yippy barks. THE PUPPIES! Streaker and Mouse had found them. They were inside!

I gave Tina a high five and whooped with triumph. It was a bit too early to celebrate, though, because we couldn't actually get into the garage. It was locked solid with a fat padlock on the door and there was no way we could make it budge.

'At least we know where they are,' said Tina excitedly. 'We can come back this afternoon before five and hide somewhere. We'll lie in wait for Charlie and catch him red-handed.'

'Sure. But we'll need to photograph it all for evidence. We need to snap him taking the puppies from the garage *and* handing them over – so no flash this time, or he'll find out.'

We made the rest of the journey home safely and in high spirits. Tina headed back to her house and I went to my room to think. I considered telling Mum and Dad but they'd only take over and where was the satisfaction in that? I wanted this to be me and Tina. Our business with Charlie was personal and we were going to take him down! On the other hand, a bit of help could be useful. Charlie and his dogs were scary.

Lunch seemed to drag on for hours. My head was spinning with my dilemma. Should I say something? Should I keep quiet?

'I suppose whoever has taken the pups has done us a small favour, really,' said Dad. That astonished me, to say the least. How on earth did Dad figure that out?

'How come?' I asked.

'We don't have to bother to find homes for them,' he said. 'And don't look at me like that, Trevor, as if I've just murdered them. I'm just trying to find something positive in all this. I've taken the card down from the post office since there doesn't seem much point in advertising something we no longer have. We'll not find them.'

I pushed my knife and fork together. I was about to tell Dad that actually he was completely wrong and Tina and I knew where they were and we were going to rescue them, SO THERE, when Dad opened his big mouth again.

'I know it's upsetting, Trev, but we have to be realistic. What are the chances of us finding those puppies? Practically zero. They could be anywhere. It's not even worth looking.'

That was the decider. Tina and I would do it on our own and show everyone.

Tina called round in the middle of the

afternoon. She had a small backpack slung over one shoulder. 'Supplies,' she explained.

'Like what?'

'Camera, torch, cos it'll be dark by five, Dictaphone for recording, can of cream –'

'Idiot!'

'I thought your thumb might still be sore.' Tina grinned.

'Ha ha. Anything else?'

Her eyes lit up. 'Bar of chocolate.'

'Great,' I said, although I couldn't understand why she was waving it in front of my nose. I reached inside my pocket, brought out a tube and held it up for Tina to see. 'I've got something too,' I announced proudly. 'Shoe polish.'

Tina glanced at our shoes in bewilderment. 'Do they need polishing?'

'It's for our faces. It'll be good camouflage in the dark.'

Tina scowled. 'Urgh! Haven't you had enough of being mucky?'

'Tina, we are going on a dangerous mission to rescue Streaker's puppies from a tough gangster and the less Charlie can see of us, the better.' I slipped the tube back in my pocket. 'OK, let's go.'

As we slipped out of the front door with Streaker, Dad saw us. 'Where are you two off to?'

'We're still looking for the puppies,' Tina answered.

'It's too late. We'll never find them now. You're

wasting your time,' Dad told her. Tina and I exchanged knowing glances and set off for our appointment with the puppies, and quite possibly Death at the hands of Charlie Smugg.

9. Attack! Attack!

We reached the lock-ups and went straight to
the puppies. As soon as they heard our voices
and Streaker scrabbling at the door they came
to the other side, yipping and yapping like crazy.
We could hear their little paws scraping away at
the metal in a useless attempt to escape. It was
heartbreaking.

Tina rummaged around in her bag and
produced the Dictaphone. She held the little
machine to the garage door and recorded the
puppies. She added some whispered comments.

'I am standing outside the padlocked door
of number seven garage. The noises you are
listening to belong to three stolen puppies that
have been locked away here by Charlie Smugg.
We are now waiting for Charlie to collect them.

He intends to sell them off for Christmas but Trevor and I are going to stop him. This is Tina and Trevor reporting from number seven lock-up. Now it's back to the studio.'

'What studio?' I asked.

'It's what reporters say when they've finished reporting,' Tina murmured.

'You're bonkers,' I muttered, handing her the shoe polish. 'Here, rub it all over your face.'

'After you,' Tina replied, watching me smear black across my cheeks, nose, chin and round my eyes. I handed her the little tub and she promptly stuck the lid on very firmly and gave it back.

'You're welcome to look like an idiot,' she said. 'I have my pride.'

'If Charlie spots you, everything will be ruined.'

'Well, he won't spot me because we are going to hide behind those old boxes and crates.'

Tina pointed out a pile of junk nearby, still coated with a powdering of snow. It wasn't a comfortable place to be and Streaker didn't want to settle at all. She was determined to dig a hole right through the concrete and into that garage to free her pups. When she wasn't allowed to do that she began barking and then howling.

'Awhooooo! Aaaaaaaaawhooooooooooooooo!!'

'For heaven's sake,' I said. 'Keep quiet, or Charlie will know we're here.'

'Ahhhwhoooooooo!'

Tina fished about in her backpack again and this time she produced a packet of dog biscuits. 'They're Mouse's. I don't suppose he'll mind.' She put a few on the ground next to us and

Streaker snaffled them as if she hadn't been fed for a month.

We squatted behind the boxes and waited. Then we waited some more. It was very boring. Tina got out the chocolate.

'Fancy some?'

'Sure.'

'Do you remember what Sharon said to Charlie?' Tina asked. I shook my head. 'She said he could have some more chocolate.' Tina's eyes were fixed on mine.

'So?' I asked, puzzled.

'She was bribing him,' Tina went on.

'Bribing him?' I was even more puzzled.

Tina sighed and rolled her eyes in despair. 'Sharon gave Charlie chocolate and he gave her –' She broke off.

'Gave her what?' I almost shouted, and then the penny dropped. 'Tina, I am NOT giving you a kiss.'

'But it's Christmas.'

'Christmas, not Kissmas,' I pointed out.

'No chocolate for you then,' she answered huffily.

'Fine. Eat it all yourself.'

'I will. Look. Yum yum yum. Ooooh, it's so lovely. Don't you want some, Trevor?'

I gritted my teeth and shook my head.

'Mmmmmmmm, it's so smooth and melty and chocolatey and warm and all gooey. Are you sure you don't want some? Yum yum yum.'

'Ssshhh!' I hissed. 'Charlie is coming – look!' It was the first time ever that I was actually pleased to see Charlie Smugg. He'd just saved me from a fate worse than death!

We hastily ducked back down behind the boxes and I clamped a hand round Streaker's muzzle. As I squeezed her mouth shut a half-chewed dog biscuit came shooting out, whizzed across the driveway and pinged against a garage door on the far side. Fortunately Charlie didn't notice. Streaker looked a bit miffed but at least she didn't struggle.

Charlie stepped
up to number seven
lock-up. He looked
all around and then
produced a small
bunch of keys. Tina
lifted her camera.

'Is the flash off?' I
whispered. She nodded
and took two or three
pictures as Charlie
undid the padlock and
rolled up the door. I
waited for the pups to
come bouncing out,
but it seemed Charlie
had kept them tethered
inside. They could
move around but they
couldn't run free.

CLICK
CLICK

'We'll have to wait until he's got them right out of the garage,' I murmured.

There was a deep rumbling noise, getting nearer. An old battered car with half its exhaust missing swung on to the driveway between the garages. It stopped near Charlie and an unpleasant-looking man got out. He had a baseball cap pulled low over his forehead. He was overweight and his belly hung so far over his belt it looked in danger of falling right off and plopping on to the floor.

'He looks as if he's swallowed a giant Christmas pudding,' Tina whispered into my ear. I nodded and watched as Pudding Man hitched up his jeans for the umpteenth time.

'Charlie?' he growled.

'Yeah. The pups are in here. All in good nick, see?' Charlie picked up one of the pups to show the man but it nipped his hand so he hastily put it back down.

The big man laughed. 'You've obviously got a knack with animals.'

Charlie scowled and said the pups weren't used to being handled. 'Do you want them or not?' he asked.

'Sure. They'll be great presents for my triplets – one each.' Pudding Man pulled a wad of notes from his back pocket and counted out some money. He handed it over to Charlie, who stood there grinning at it while Tina quietly took another snap.

'Put 'em in the back of the car,' said the man.

Charlie began to undo the puppies' leads, ready for transfer. I grabbed Tina's arm.

'We've got to do something. We have to stop this happening right now before those puppies get taken away and we lose them again.'

'What are you going to do?' she asked.

'I don't know!'

My brain had gone into meltdown. I couldn't think. I was frozen to the spot and the puppies were being taken away right under my nose. But while Tina and I just sat there, desperately wondering what to do, Streaker had come up with a plan of her own and I think it was called: ATTACK! ATTACK!

Charlie emerged from the garage with the three puppies struggling in his arms. It was more than Streaker could bear. She leaped out from behind the crates, legs in a whirling blur. She rocketed straight at him, trailing a long, unearthly howl behind as she whizzed through the air.

'Whooooooooooooooooooooooo!!!'

Streaker hit Charlie hard and square and he doubled over, spilling the pups on to the ground. Tina and I dashed out and scooped them into our arms.

'You get back here!' yelled Charlie. 'Stop, thief!'

'Run for it!' yelled Tina.

'Oi!' bellowed Pudding Man. 'Them's my dogs! Come back! I've paid for them!'

The pair of them came racing after us and it was obvious who could run faster. For a start we were laden down with three puppies who seemed to think it was all great fun. One of mine was trying to lick my face while I ran. The other was attempting to make death-defying leaps without a parachute from my arms. Tina's pup appeared to be burrowing down inside her coat. All I could see was a short tail sticking out of the top by her neck, wagging furiously.

Charlie and Pudding Man were catching up rapidly. That was when Streaker came racing

to the rescue. She hurtled after the two thieves,
nipping at their ankles, bouncing, leaping, darting
between their legs and generally getting in their
way.

First of all Charlie went crashing to the ground
as he tripped right over her and then Streaker
pulled off her most spectacular trick of all. Flying

along beside Pudding Man, she leaped up at his
legs. Her teeth closed on the man's jeans and the
next moment they were down round his ankles
and he fell, flat on his face! Bang!

Tina and I yelled with delight and turned
towards the town. Streaker soon caught us up
and danced along beside us, her ears flapping like

happy flags as she barked with delight – it almost sounded like laughter. She was so pleased to have her pups back.

However, we still had a long way to go before we reached home. We went as fast as we could, but we hadn't even reached the centre of town when we heard the angry roar of a speeding car with a missing exhaust. They were coming after us IN THE CAR! There was no way Streaker could trip that up!

10. The Great Switch-On

'I'm getting a stitch,' Tina cried.

'Shouldn't have eaten that chocolate,' I shouted
back. 'Come on! If we can get to the centre
there'll be too many people around for Charlie to
get at us.'

We heard the car spit gravel as it zoomed away
from the lock-ups and came tearing down the
road.

'Come on!' I yelled, but Tina was bent double,
eyes screwed up in pain.

'You go, take this one,' she panted, handing
over the last puppy. I glanced up the road at the
monster roaring towards us. We were so near
to making it to safety and yet so far. If only we
could reach the next corner the market square
would be in sight, full of people waiting to see the

Christmas lights switched on. I pulled at Tina's arm.

'Tina, you can do it. Keep walking.'

Tina straightened up, still clutching her side. I practically pulled her along the road but I knew we weren't going to make it. We still had a hundred metres or so to the corner when the car thundered up alongside us and screeched to a halt. The driver's door flew open and Pudding Man lifted himself out, his face a red, raging beetroot.

'You've got my dogs!' he spat.

'They're my dogs!' I yelled back.

'You'd better hand them over before I turn you to paste!' the man growled. The passenger door opened and Charlie started to get out.

In the distance a siren started up. Pudding Man pricked up his ears. He hesitated and stared up the road. A flashing blue light squealed round the corner and raced towards us. Charlie yelled across in a panic.

'Get back in! Go! Go!'

Pudding Man dived back into the car, gunned the engine and skidded away, the car snaking down to the corner and lurching round. The police car went zooming past, lights flashing, siren blaring and – oh boy! Sergeant Smugg was at the wheel! Sergeant Smugg was chasing his own son!

Tina and I looked at each other and then ran as fast as we could to the corner. We wanted to see what was happening. We got there just in time to see the mayor standing on a platform

PAH! PAH!

beside the big Christmas tree, ready to start the countdown, while Charlie's car tried to push its way through the heaving crowd.

'And now it's the big switch-on,' cried the mayor. 'We'll count down from five and here we go: FIVE, FOUR, THREE, TWO, ONE – ta da!' The lights flickered on. Everywhere coloured lights began twinkling. Lovely!

PAH! PAH! hooted Charlie's car as it forced its

way through. Pudding Man was hanging out of
the window, trying to push people out of the way
with one hand and steer with the other.

'Get out the way!' he yelled. 'Move, you idiots!
I'm in a hurry! I've got a pregnant woman on
board about to have a baby – get out the way!
What are you – cows? Sheep? Baaa baaa mooo –
go on, move it!'

PAH! PAH!

And right behind came Sergeant Smugg, making even more noise.

DEE DOO DEE DOO DEE DOO!

It was complete chaos. Deeper and deeper into the crowd went the fleeing car until, with one final surge, it plunged straight into the base of the giant Christmas tree and could go no further.

The tree wobbled. It wibbled. It probably even wubbled. And then it slowly started to topple. Slowly, slowly, then faster and faster until it came crashing down. And as it fell it sliced through one of the main strings of bulbs stretched between the lamp posts. Sparks flew in every direction, bulbs smashed and suddenly ALL the Christmas lights went out.

Finally the tree hit the ground, bringing down the lights with it and bending several lamp posts into strange angles at the same time.

The doors of Charlie's car opened and out they climbed. Charlie was shouting angrily at Pudding Man saying that no way was he a

pregnant woman. Pudding Man yelled back
that everything was Charlie's fault. They tried
desperately to escape but the angry crowd seized
them and held them tight. Sergeant Smugg
stopped his car and strode across.

'I arrest the pair of you!' he declared proudly,
as if he'd done all the catching by himself. He
laid a hand on Charlie's shoulder and swung him
round so that they were face to face. I don't know
who was more shocked.

'Charlie?!'

'Dad?'

Several people in the crowd began to laugh. They obviously knew Charlie only too well, not to mention his father. This was justice at last. Charlie and Pudding Man were put in the back of the patrol car and a red-faced Sergeant Smugg drove them away to the police station.

Tina and I were over the moon – and so was Streaker. Just for once she hadn't caused all the mayhem in the town centre. Not only that, she had her beloved puppies back and did she make a fuss of them? She certainly did!

We took them all back home. Mum and Dad were HUGELY surprised and, I'm pleased to say, they were pretty happy too. This was going to be the best Christmas ever. We would all be together after all – me, Mum, Dad, Streaker AND the puppies. I knew that the puppies would soon go to new homes in January, but at least I had them for Christmas.

Later that evening Tina and I went over the whole business.

'It's been brilliant,' I said.

'I know. And you were amazing. You could have left me behind, but you didn't.'

I shrugged and Tina fished around in one of her pockets. 'What are you after now?' I asked.

'I'm just looking for something. I got you a little present to say thank you.'

'Oh?'

'Yes, I found it when everything fell over in the market this afternoon. Ah, here it is.'

Tina proudly produced her present and held it up high. I gulped. Mistletoe. Was there no escape?

10½. The Very Last Bit

We discovered a few days after Christmas that Charlie just about got away with it. He'd told his dad that he'd 'found' the puppies, so how was he to know who they belonged to?

What's more, Charlie was still threatening to take money off Tina and me. Fortunately we had already come up with a plan for this, just in case. Tina handed Charlie an envelope.

'What is it?' he asked suspiciously, as well he might.

Tina shrugged. 'Take a look.'

Charlie stuck a grubby thumb into one corner of the envelope and ripped it open. He pulled out a single sheet of paper. He looked at the photo and gasped. The blood drained from his face.

Tina and I grinned. 'If you make any more

trouble for us,' I said, 'you will find a copy of that photo taped to every lamp post in this town.'

We left Charlie standing there, stunned and shaken. We'd only gone a few paces when Tina turned back.

'Happy Christmas, Charlie!' she chuckled. 'And to Sharon Blenkinsop too!'

And I thought, yeah, too right. Happy Christmas, Charlie!

Ask Jeremy

Of all the books you have written, which one is your favourite?

I loved writing both **KRAZY KOW SAVES THE WORLD – WELL, ALMOST** and **STUFF**, my first book for teenagers. Both these made me laugh out loud while I was writing and I was pleased with the overall result in each case. I also love writing the stories about Nicholas and his daft family – **MY DAD**, **MY MUM**, **MY BROTHER** and so on.

If you couldn't be a writer what would you be?

Well, I'd be pretty fed up for a start, because writing was the one thing I knew I wanted to do from the age of nine onward. But if I DID have to do something else, I would love to be either an accomplished pianist or an artist of some sort. Music and art have played a big part in my whole life and I would love to be involved in them in some way.

What's the best thing about writing stories?

Oh dear – so many things to say here! Getting paid for making things up is pretty high on the list! It's also something you do on your own, inside your own head – nobody can interfere with that. The only boss you have is yourself. And you are creating something that nobody else has made before you. I also love making my readers laugh and want to read more and more.

Did you ever have a nightmare teacher? (And who was your best ever?)

My nightmare at primary school was Mrs Chappell, long since dead. I knew her secret – she was not actually human. She was a Tyrannosaurus rex in disguise. She taught me for two years when I was in Y5 and Y6, and we didn't like each other at all. My best ever was when I was in Y3 and Y4. Her name was Miss Cox, and she was the one who first encouraged me to write stories. She was brilliant. Sadly, she is long dead too.

When you were a kid you used to play kiss-chase. Did you always do the chasing or did anyone ever chase you?!

I usually did the chasing, but when I got chased, I didn't bother to run very fast! Maybe I shouldn't admit to that! We didn't play kiss-chase at school – it was usually played during holidays. If we had tried playing it at school we would have been in serious trouble. Mind you, I seemed to spend most of my time in trouble of one sort or another, so maybe it wouldn't have mattered that much.

It all started with a Scarecrow

Puffin is well over sixty years old.
Sounds ancient, doesn't it? But Puffin has never been
so lively. We're always on the lookout for the next big
idea, which is how it began all those years ago.

Penguin Books was a big idea from the mind of
a man called Allen Lane, who in 1935 invented
the quality paperback and changed the world.
**And from great Penguins, great Puffins grew,
changing the face of children's books forever.**

The first four Puffin Picture Books were hatched in 1940 and the
first Puffin story book featured a man with broomstick arms called
Worzel Gummidge. In 1967 Kaye Webb, Puffin Editor, started the
Puffin Club, promising to **'make children into readers'**.
She kept that promise and over 200,000 children became
devoted Puffineers through their quarterly instalments of
Puffin Post, which is now back for a new generation.

Many years from now, we hope you'll look back and
remember Puffin with a smile. **No matter what your age
or what you're into, there's a Puffin for everyone.**
The possibilities are endless, but one thing is for sure:
whether it's a picture book or a paperback, a sticker book
or a hardback, **if it's got that little Puffin
on it – it's bound to be good.**